Copyright © 2015 by Levi Pinfold

All rights reserved. No part of this book may be reproduced, transmitted, or
stored in an information retrieval system in any form or by any means, graphic,
electronic, or mechanical, including photocopying, taping, and recording,
without prior written permission from the publisher.

First U.S. edition 2016

Library of Congress Catalog Card Number 2014939341
ISBN 978-0-7636-7598-1

TTP 20 19 18 17 16 15
10 9 8 7 6 5 4 3 2 1
Printed in Huizhou, Guangdong, China

This book was typeset in Adobe Caslon Regular.
The illustrations were done in mixed media.

TEMPLAR BOOKS

an imprint of
Candlewick Press
99 Dover Street
Somerville, Massachusetts 02144
www.candlewick.com

GREENLING by LEVI PINFOLD

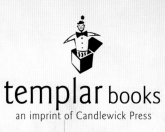

templar books
an imprint of Candlewick Press

What is this growing on Barleycorn land?

What is this standing, where once stood a tree?

Is it intended for Barleycorn hands?

I wonder, thinks he, could this be for me?

His wife wants to know where it came from.

He says, "Where the wildflowers grow."

She says, "It belongs to the wild, then,

and back to the land it should go."

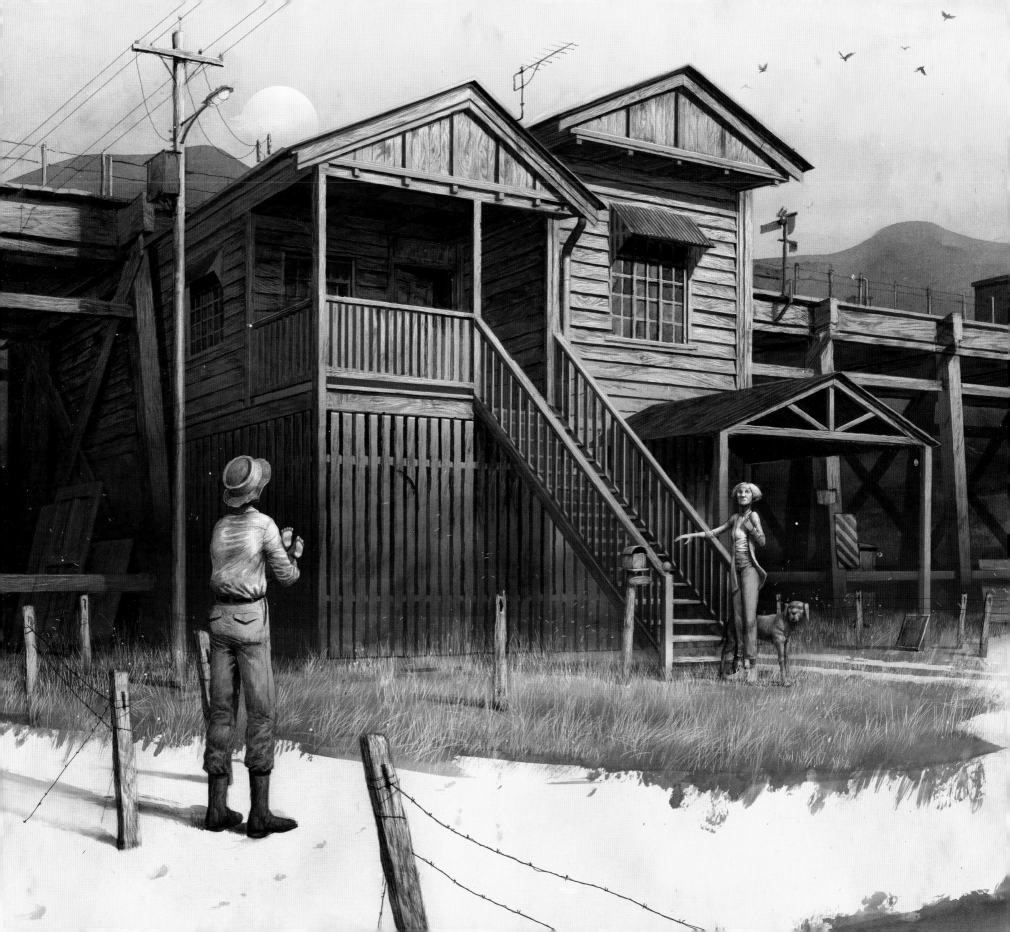

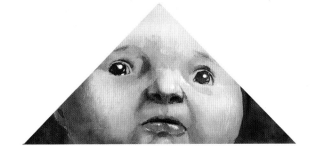

You cannot return for a refund.

A baby is not like a hat.

What's picked is picked, what's done is done,

and that, Barleycorns, is that.

So forget what you know about baby demands.

This is a different breed.

It's clear he has needs only trees understand,

a vegetable hunger to feed.

With night fast approaching Barleycorn says,

"We can't leave him outside for the crows.

If some of this outside were inside,

he could settle in safe, if he chose."

"I know what you're up to," mutters his wife,

"but keeping him here is not right.

Get rid of this goblin by morning.

He goes, or we're in for a fight."

But morning brings stranger becomings, beginning a Barleycorn gripe.

She says, "How will we cook breakfast today?" He says, "Them melons look ripe."

She retreats to the sofa to lie down, but her hopes of a rest take a blow.

She says, "How will we watch TV tonight?" He says, "Just look at him grow."

Escaping the house is no option; the transport has taken to seed.

She says, "Well, there goes the shopping!" He says, "Depends what you need . . ."

"We've got pumpkins and peppers, spring onions and sage,

apples more golden than money.

Why would we want to pile more on our plate,

when we're already swimming in honey?"

"Dear husband," she says, "what are you? A bee?!

You're beginning to buzz like a drone.

I'm calling for help to fix up your brain."

But grass has invaded the phone.

Retreating in rage to her bedroom,

Mrs. Barleycorn's opted to flee.

Whatever will happen tonight? she thinks.

Why now? Why here? Why me?

A screech of brakes awakes her at dawn, then humming up on the lines . . .

A swarm of passengers, bound for work, are stopped in their tracks by vines.

"That creature must go!" says a voice in the crowd.
"He's pushing us out of our world!
These people all need to be moving along—
this vegetable must be hurled."

Well, that's not right, Mrs. Barleycorn thinks,
the boy is just strange, not bad . . .
A baby's a baby, when all's said and done,
there's no need for them to get mad.

Thoughts boiling over, she bellows aloud,
"I think you've gotten it wrong.
We should welcome this Greenling into our house,
we've been living in his all along!"

Suddenly flowering with all the attention,

Greenling sits up and speaks;

an old magic word, long since forgotten,

casts an odd spell for weeks . . .

They eat up the apples, the mangoes and plums, they eat up the oranges too.

They eat up the fruit of the Greenling, fruit much too good to be true.

So a long summer begins and continues:
a harvest with each morning light.
Strange and enchanted Greenling cuisine
has everyone filled with delight.

But all summer things must come to an end
when the summer days are done.
As autumn arrives, the Barleycorns find
that Greenling has left with the sun.

Barleycorn says, "He's a Greenling.
Who can say what they intend?
He left us with this for the winter,
but I don't think this is the end . . ."

What do the hills and the trees have planned?

Does Mr. Barleycorn quite understand?

When winter has passed, and spring is to hand . . .

What will be growing on Barleycorn land?